W9-CLJ-532

HAN SOLO: VOLUME 2

It is a period of unrest. In a galaxy oppressed by the Empire's merciless cruelty, there is little hope for the future. Nonetheless, rebels have banded together to fight back against such corruption.

Untrusting by nature, Han Solo has taken a step back from the rebel cause, returning his focus to what he does best – smuggling. However, when Princess Leia approaches him with an offer too good to refuse, Han finds himself once again working for the Rebellion alongside his co-pilot, Chewbacca.

His mission is racing the Millennium Falcon in one of the most notorious races in the galaxy, the Dragon Void, as a cover to find a mysterious rebel spy who may have turned traitor. But with the race's explosive start, Han discovers he may be in for more than he bargained for....

MARJORIE LIU
Writer

MARK BROOKS
Pencils

DEXTER VINES
Inks

SONIA OBACK
Colors

LEE BERMEJO
Cover Artist

VC's JOE CARAMAGNA
Letterer

HEATHER ANTOS
Assistant Editor

JORDAN D. WHITE
Editor

C.B. CEBULSKI
Executive Editor

AXEL ALONSO
Editor In Chief

JOE QUESADA
Chief Creative Officer

DAN BUCKLEY
Publisher

For Lucasfilm:
Creative Director **MICHAEL SIGLAIN**
Senior Editor **FRANK PARISI**
Lucasfilm Story Group **RAYNE ROBERTS, PABLO HIDALGO, LELAND CHEE, MATT MARTIN**

ABDO
Spotlight

ABDOPUBLISHING.COM

Reinforced library bound edition published in 2018 by Spotlight,
a division of ABDO, PO Box 398166, Minneapolis, Minnesota 55439.
Spotlight produces high-quality reinforced library bound editions for
schools and libraries. Published by agreement with Marvel Characters, Inc.

Printed in the United States of America, North Mankato, Minnesota.
042017
092017

THIS BOOK CONTAINS
RECYCLED MATERIALS

marvelkids.com

PUBLISHER'S CATALOGING IN PUBLICATION DATA

Names: Liu, Marjorie, author. | Brooks, Mark ; Oback, Sonia ; Milla, Matt,
    illustrators.
Title: Han Solo / writer: Marjorie Liu ; art: Mark Brooks ; Sonia Oback ; Matt Milla.
Description: Reinforced library bound edition. | Minneapolis, Minnesota : Spotlight,
    2018. | Series: Star wars : Han Solo | Volumes 1, 2, 3, and 5 written by Marjorie
    Liu ; illustrated by Mark Brooks, & Sonia Oback. | Volume 4 written by Marjorie
    Liu ; illustrated by Mark Brooks, Sonia Oback, & Matt Milla.
Summary: When Princess Leia approaches him with an offer too good to refuse,
    Han Solo finds himself flying in one of the galaxy's most dangerous races, the
    Dragon Void, as a cover to find a mysterious rebel spy who may have turned
    traitor.
Identifiers: LCCN 2017931205 | ISBN 9781532140150 (volume 1) | ISBN
    9781532140167 (volume 2) | ISBN 9781532140174 (volume 3) | ISBN
    9781532140181 (volume 4) | ISBN 9781532140198 (volume 5)
Subjects: LCSH: Solo, Han (Fictitious character)--Juvenile fiction. | Space warfare--
    Juvenile fiction. | Adventure and adventurers--Juvenile fiction. | Comic book,
    strips, etc.--Juvenile fiction. | Graphic novels--Juvenile fiction.
Classification: DDC 741.5--dc23
LC record available at https://lccn.loc.gov/2017931205

Spotlight

A Division of ABDO
abdopublishing.com

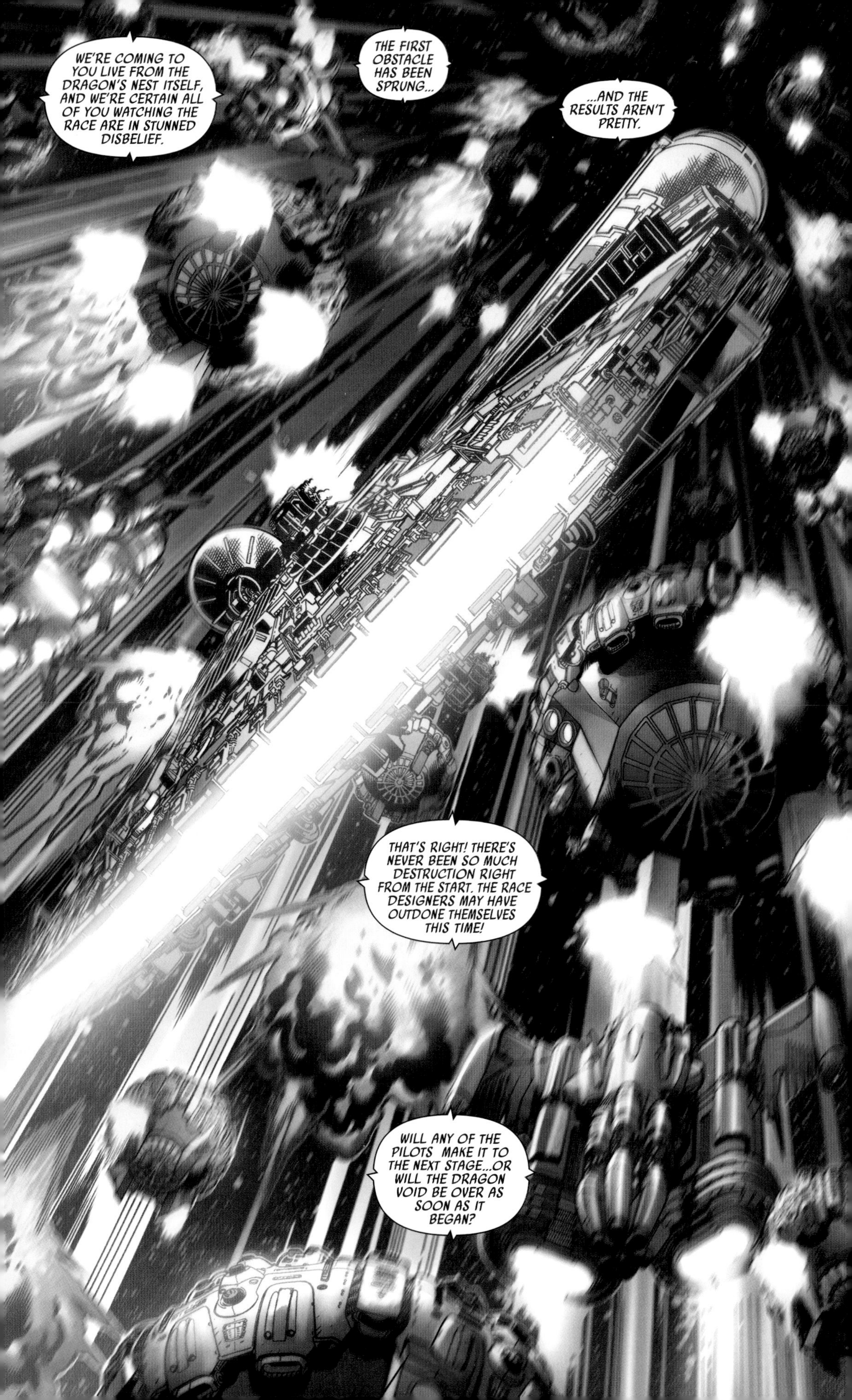
WE'RE COMING TO YOU LIVE FROM THE DRAGON'S NEST ITSELF, AND WE'RE CERTAIN ALL OF YOU WATCHING THE RACE ARE IN STUNNED DISBELIEF.
THE FIRST OBSTACLE HAS BEEN SPRUNG...
...AND THE RESULTS AREN'T PRETTY.
THAT'S RIGHT! THERE'S NEVER BEEN SO MUCH DESTRUCTION RIGHT FROM THE START. THE RACE DESIGNERS MAY HAVE OUTDONE THEMSELVES THIS TIME!
WILL ANY OF THE PILOTS MAKE IT TO THE NEXT STAGE...OR WILL THE DRAGON VOID BE OVER AS SOON AS IT BEGAN?

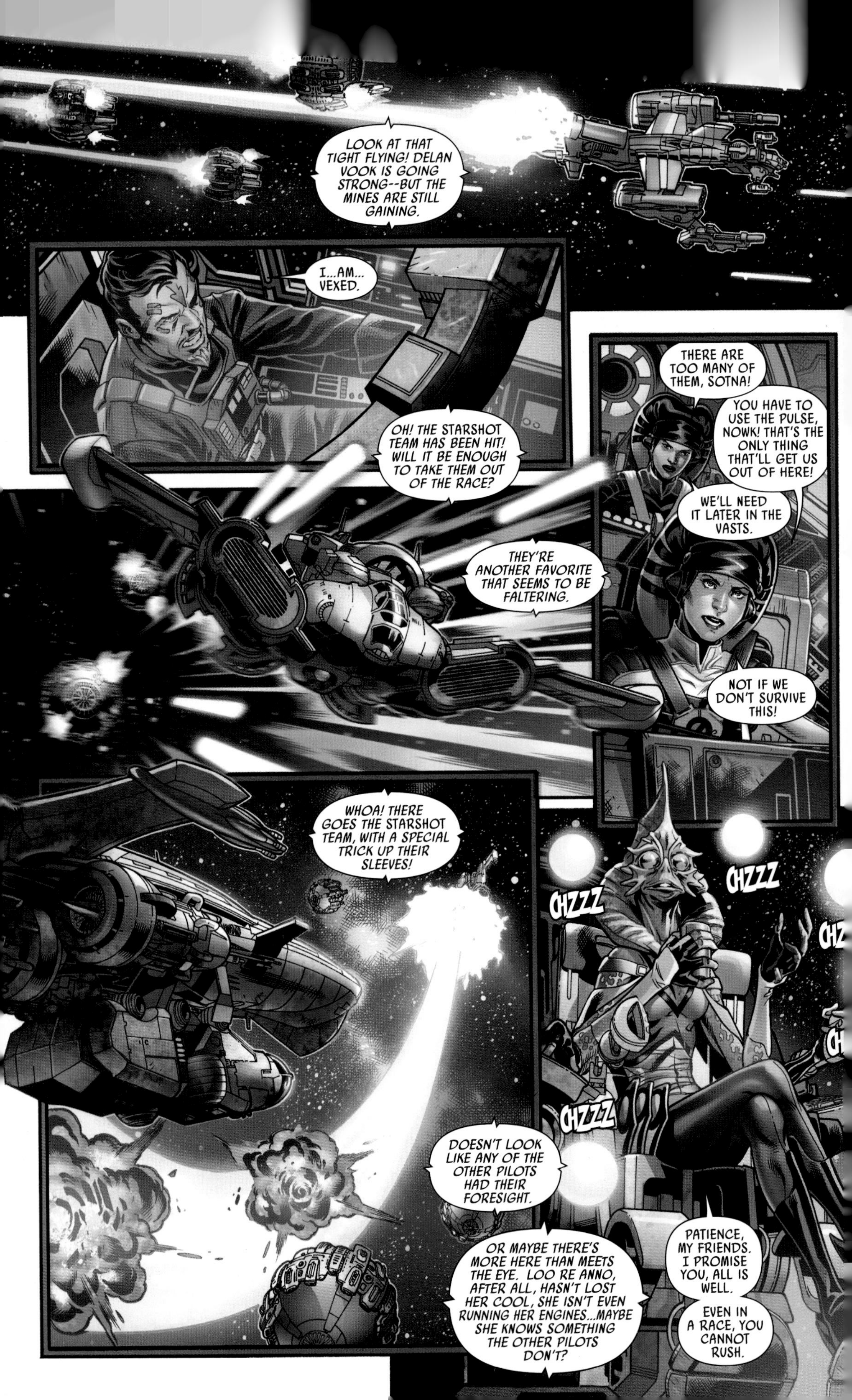
LOOK AT THAT TIGHT FLYING! DELAN VOOK IS GOING STRONG--BUT THE MINES ARE STILL GAINING.
I...AM... VEXED.
THERE ARE TOO MANY OF THEM, SOTNA!
YOU HAVE TO USE THE PULSE, NOWK! THAT'S THE ONLY THING THAT'LL GET US OUT OF HERE!
WE'LL NEED IT LATER IN THE VASTS.
NOT IF WE DON'T SURVIVE THIS!
OH! THE STARSHOT TEAM HAS BEEN HIT! WILL IT BE ENOUGH TO TAKE THEM OUT OF THE RACE?
THEY'RE ANOTHER FAVORITE THAT SEEMS TO BE FALTERING.
WHOA! THERE GOES THE STARSHOT TEAM, WITH A SPECIAL TRICK UP THEIR SLEEVES!
DOESN'T LOOK LIKE ANY OF THE OTHER PILOTS HAD THEIR FORESIGHT.
CHZZZ
CHZZZ
CHZZZ
OR MAYBE THERE'S MORE HERE THAN MEETS THE EYE. LOO RE ANNO, AFTER ALL, HASN'T LOST HER COOL, SHE ISN'T EVEN RUNNING HER ENGINES...MAYBE SHE KNOWS SOMETHING THE OTHER PILOTS DON'T?
PATIENCE, MY FRIENDS. I PROMISE YOU, ALL IS WELL.
EVEN IN A RACE, YOU CANNOT RUSH.

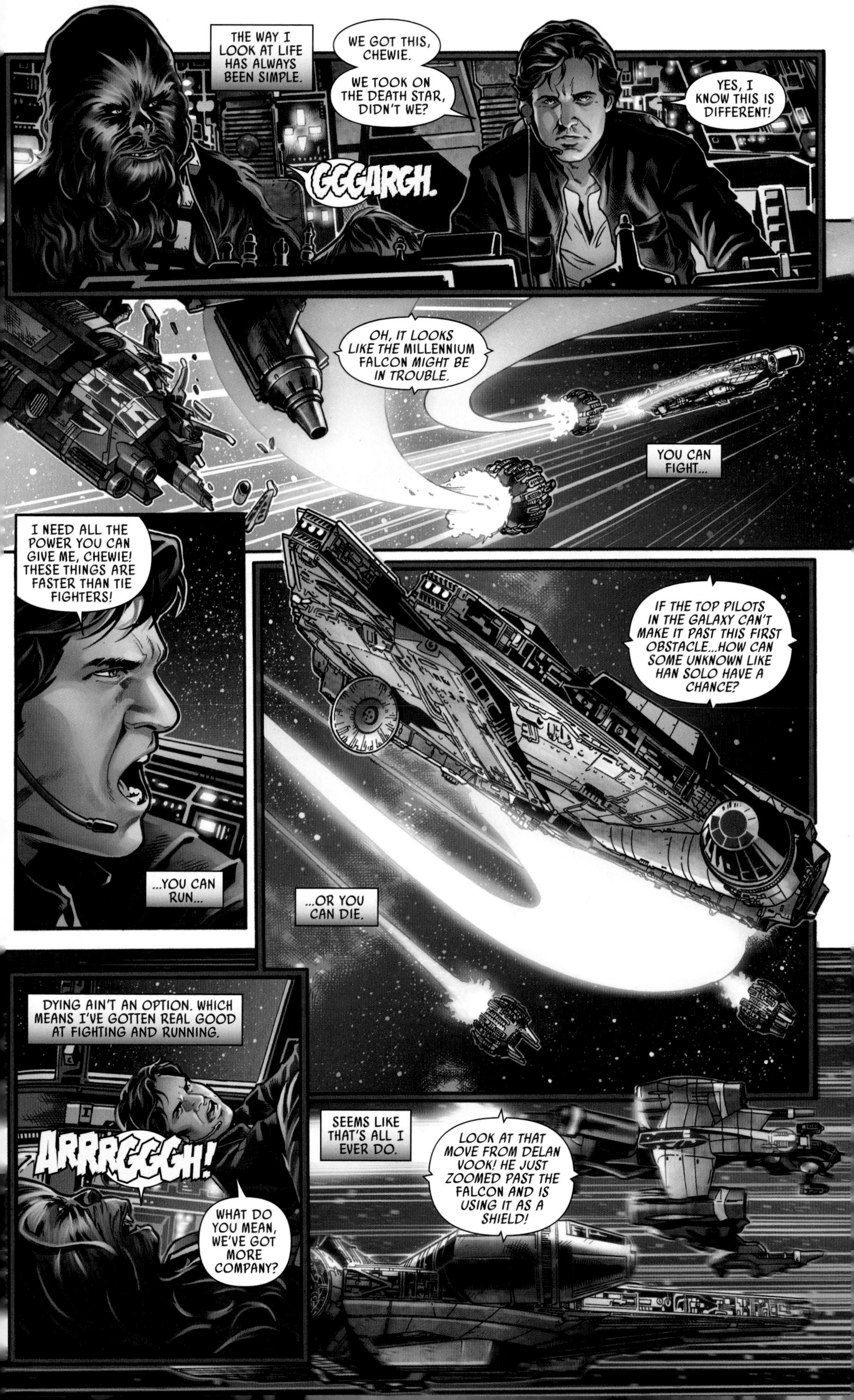
THE WAY I LOOK AT LIFE HAS ALWAYS BEEN SIMPLE.
WE GOT THIS, CHEWIE.
WE TOOK ON THE DEATH STAR, DIDN'T WE?
GGGARGH.
YES, I KNOW THIS IS DIFFERENT!
OH, IT LOOKS LIKE THE MILLENNIUM FALCON MIGHT BE IN TROUBLE.
YOU CAN FIGHT...
I NEED ALL THE POWER YOU CAN GIVE ME, CHEWIE! THESE THINGS ARE FASTER THAN TIE FIGHTERS!
...YOU CAN RUN...
IF THE TOP PILOTS IN THE GALAXY CAN'T MAKE IT PAST THIS FIRST OBSTACLE...HOW CAN SOME UNKNOWN LIKE HAN SOLO HAVE A CHANCE?
...OR YOU CAN DIE.
DYING AIN'T AN OPTION. WHICH MEANS I'VE GOTTEN REAL GOOD AT FIGHTING AND RUNNING.
ARRRGGGH!
WHAT DO YOU MEAN, WE'VE GOT MORE COMPANY?
SEEMS LIKE THAT'S ALL I EVER DO.
LOOK AT THAT MOVE FROM DELAN VOOK! HE JUST ZOOMED PAST THE FALCON AND IS USING IT AS A SHIELD!

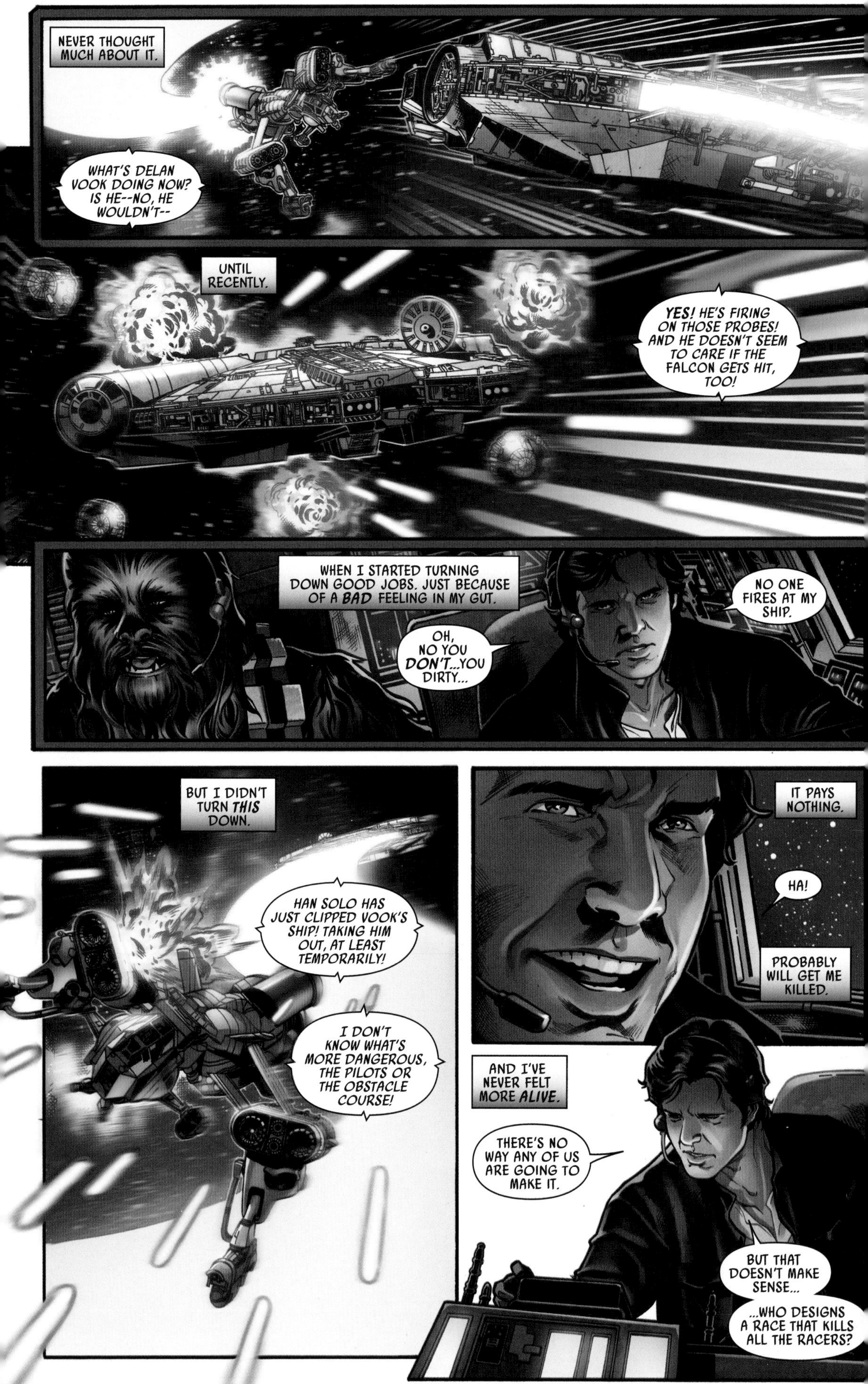
NEVER THOUGHT MUCH ABOUT IT.
WHAT'S DELAN VOOK DOING NOW? IS HE--NO, HE WOULDN'T--
UNTIL RECENTLY.
YES! HE'S FIRING ON THOSE PROBES! AND HE DOESN'T SEEM TO CARE IF THE FALCON GETS HIT, TOO!
WHEN I STARTED TURNING DOWN GOOD JOBS. JUST BECAUSE OF A BAD FEELING IN MY GUT.
NO ONE FIRES AT MY SHIP.
OH, NO YOU DON'T...YOU DIRTY...
BUT I DIDN'T TURN THIS DOWN.
HAN SOLO HAS JUST CLIPPED VOOK'S SHIP! TAKING HIM OUT, AT LEAST TEMPORARILY!
I DON'T KNOW WHAT'S MORE DANGEROUS, THE PILOTS OR THE OBSTACLE COURSE!
IT PAYS NOTHING.
HA!
PROBABLY WILL GET ME KILLED.
AND I'VE NEVER FELT MORE ALIVE.
THERE'S NO WAY ANY OF US ARE GOING TO MAKE IT.
BUT THAT DOESN'T MAKE SENSE...
...WHO DESIGNS A RACE THAT KILLS ALL THE RACERS?

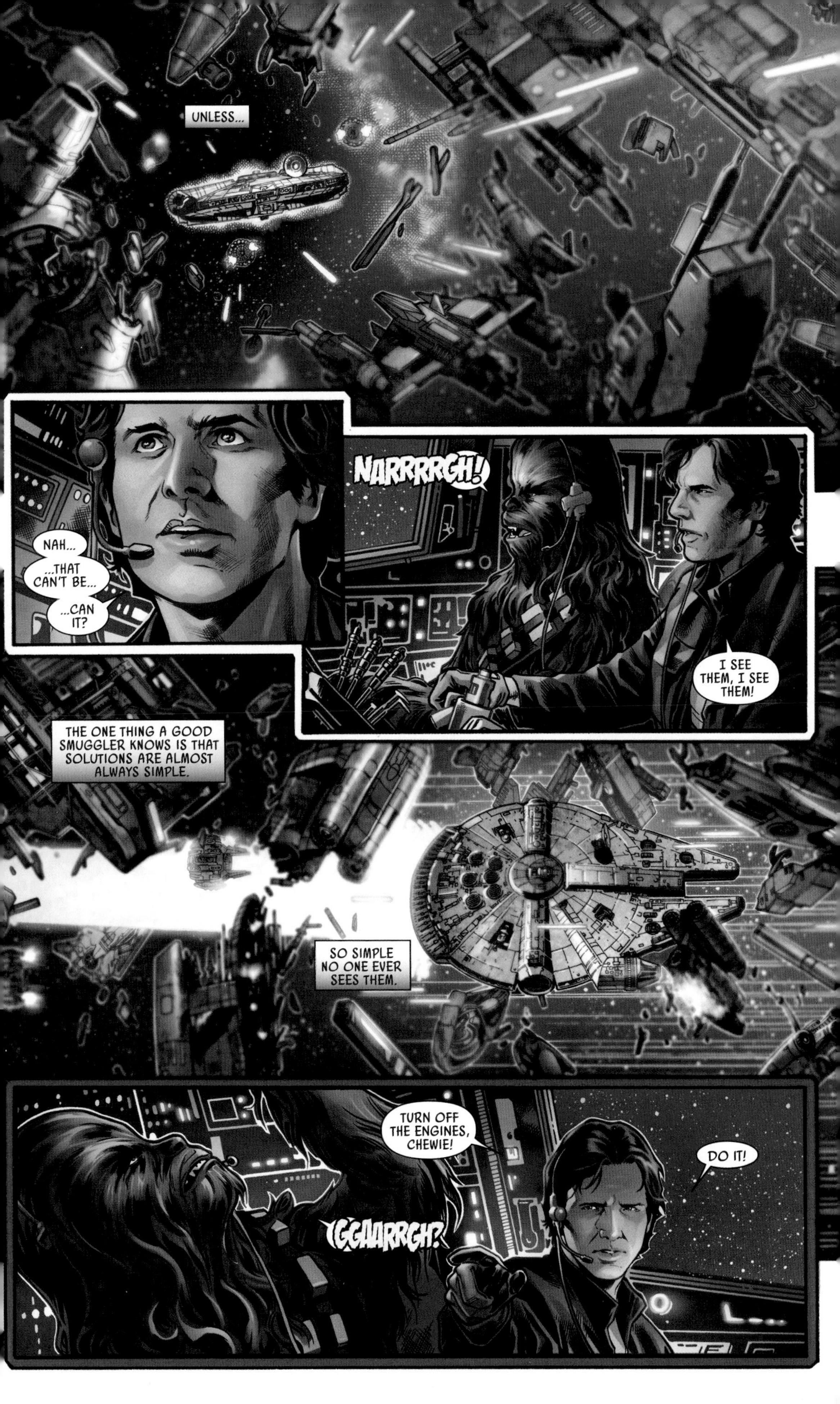
UNLESS...
NAH...
...THAT CAN'T BE...
...CAN IT?
NARRRRGH!
I SEE THEM, I SEE THEM!
THE ONE THING A GOOD SMUGGLER KNOWS IS THAT SOLUTIONS ARE ALMOST ALWAYS SIMPLE.
SO SIMPLE NO ONE EVER SEES THEM.
TURN OFF THE ENGINES, CHEWIE!
DO IT!
GGUARRGH?

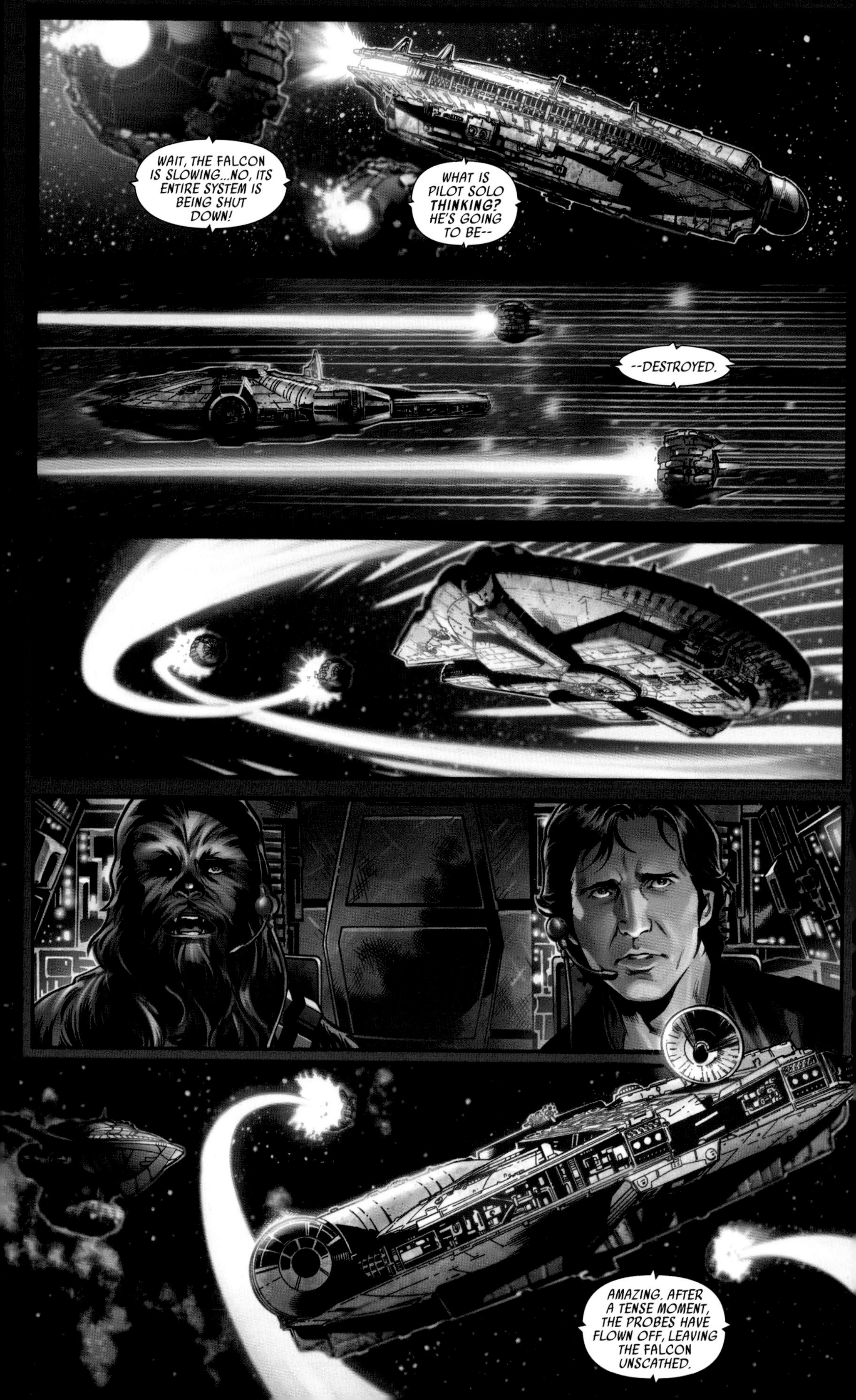

WAIT, THE FALCON IS SLOWING...NO, ITS ENTIRE SYSTEM IS BEING SHUT DOWN!
WHAT IS PILOT SOLO THINKING? HE'S GOING TO BE--
--DESTROYED.
AMAZING. AFTER A TENSE MOMENT, THE PROBES HAVE FLOWN OFF, LEAVING THE FALCON UNSCATHED.

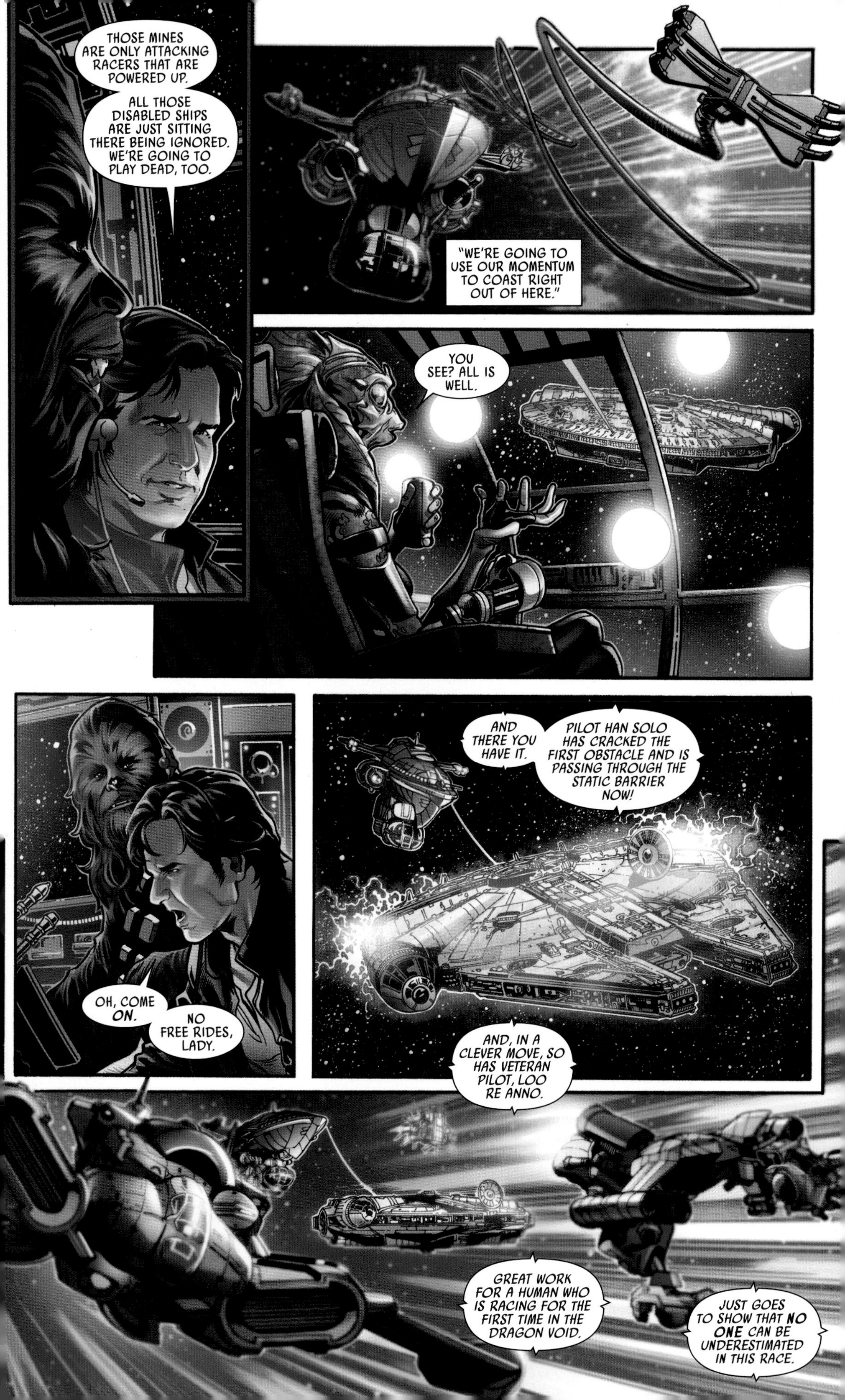
THOSE MINES ARE ONLY ATTACKING RACERS THAT ARE POWERED UP.
ALL THOSE DISABLED SHIPS ARE JUST SITTING THERE BEING IGNORED. WE'RE GOING TO PLAY DEAD, TOO.
"WE'RE GOING TO USE OUR MOMENTUM TO COAST RIGHT OUT OF HERE."
YOU SEE? ALL IS WELL.
OH, COME ON.
NO FREE RIDES, LADY.
AND THERE YOU HAVE IT.
PILOT HAN SOLO HAS CRACKED THE FIRST OBSTACLE AND IS PASSING THROUGH THE STATIC BARRIER NOW!
AND, IN A CLEVER MOVE, SO HAS VETERAN PILOT, LOO RE ANNO.
GREAT WORK FOR A HUMAN WHO IS RACING FOR THE FIRST TIME IN THE DRAGON VOID.
JUST GOES TO SHOW THAT NO ONE CAN BE UNDERESTIMATED IN THIS RACE.

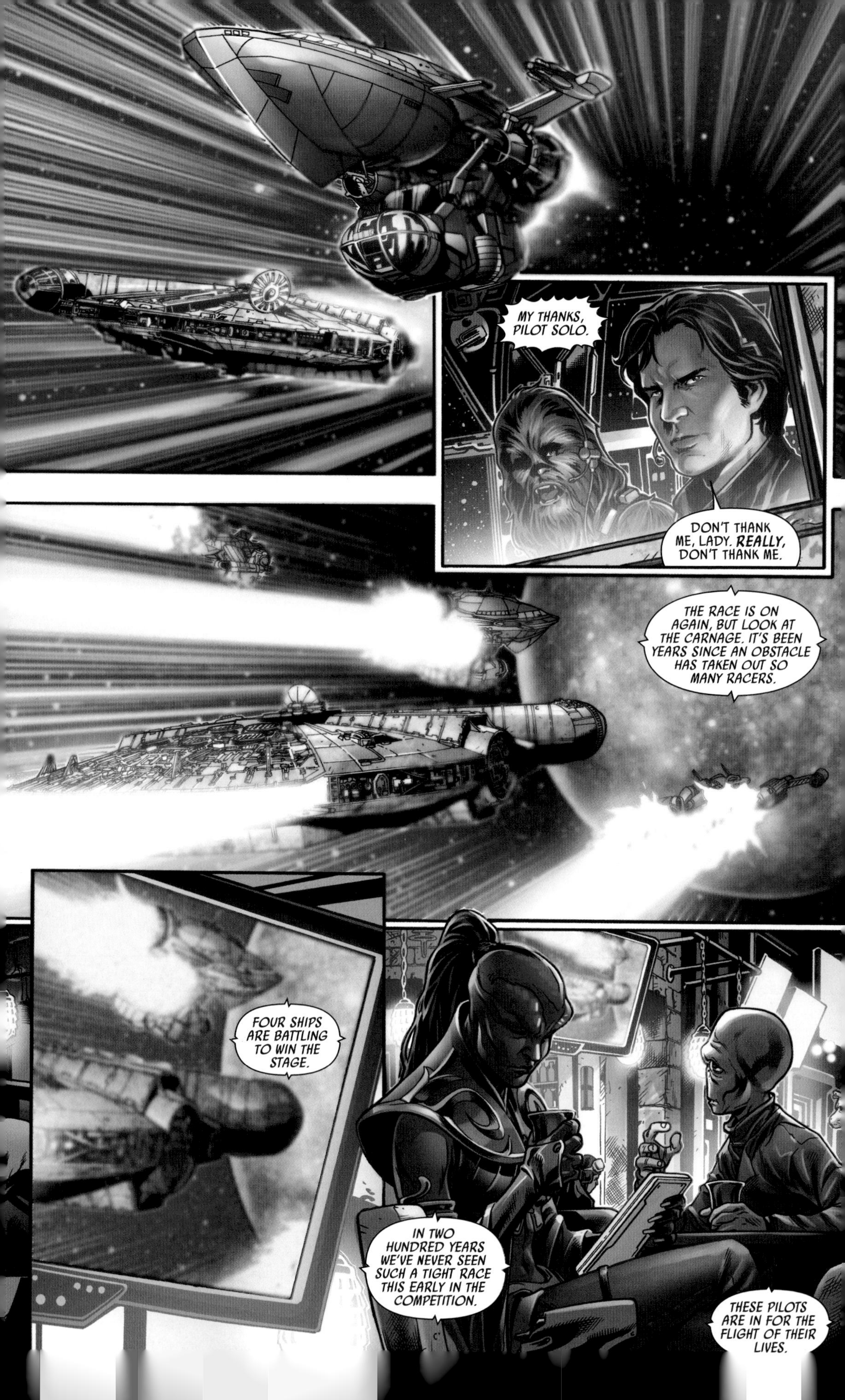
MY THANKS, PILOT SOLO.
DON'T THANK ME, LADY. REALLY, DON'T THANK ME.
THE RACE IS ON AGAIN, BUT LOOK AT THE CARNAGE. IT'S BEEN YEARS SINCE AN OBSTACLE HAS TAKEN OUT SO MANY RACERS.
FOUR SHIPS ARE BATTLING TO WIN THE STAGE.
IN TWO HUNDRED YEARS WE'VE NEVER SEEN SUCH A TIGHT RACE THIS EARLY IN THE COMPETITION.
THESE PILOTS ARE IN FOR THE FLIGHT OF THEIR LIVES.

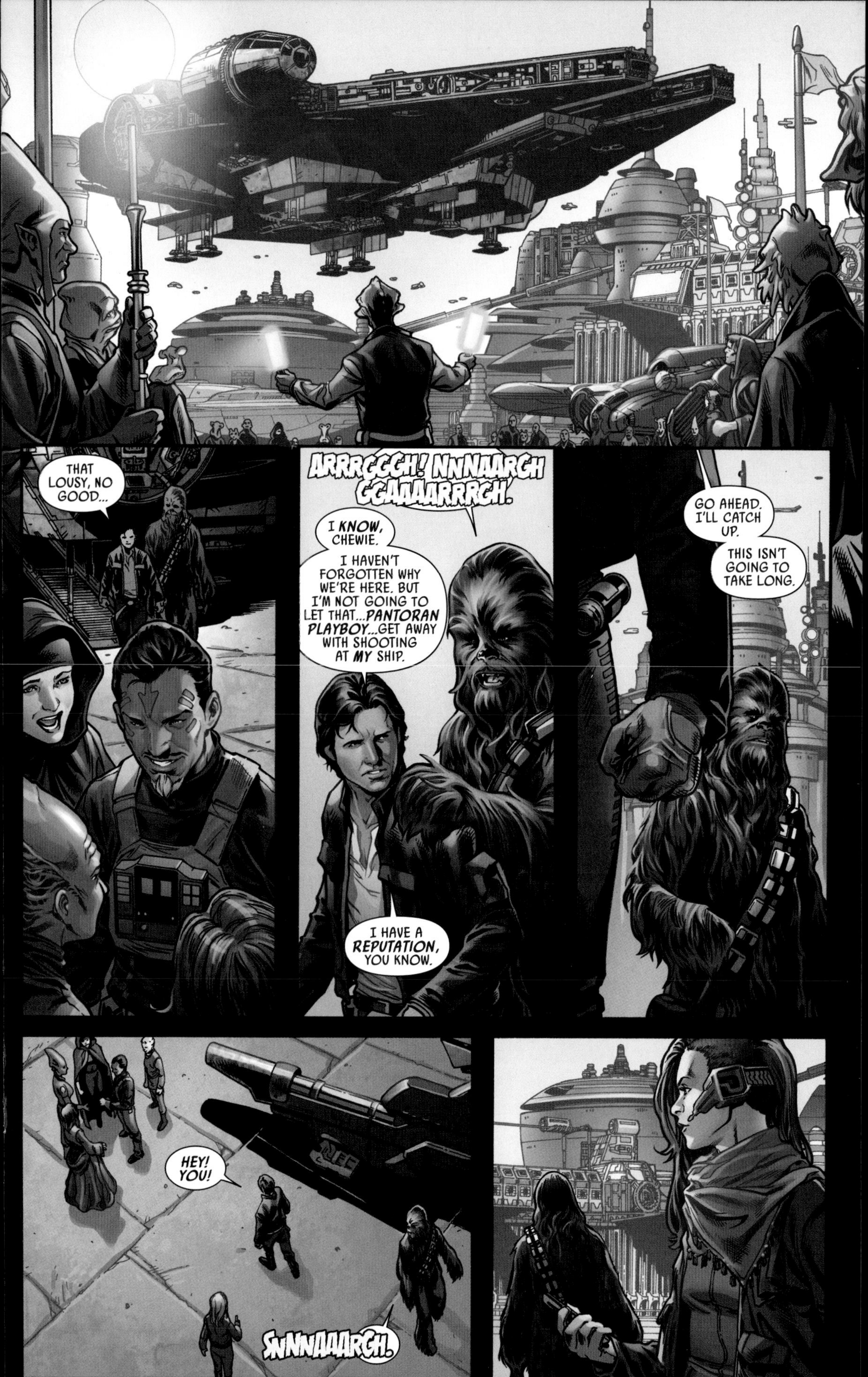
THAT LOUSY, NO GOOD...
ARRRGGGH! NNNAARGH GGAAAARRRGH.
I KNOW, CHEWIE.
I HAVEN'T FORGOTTEN WHY WE'RE HERE. BUT I'M NOT GOING TO LET THAT...PANTORAN PLAYBOY...GET AWAY WITH SHOOTING AT MY SHIP.
I HAVE A REPUTATION, YOU KNOW.
GO AHEAD. I'LL CATCH UP.
THIS ISN'T GOING TO TAKE LONG.
HEY! YOU!
SNNNAAARGH.

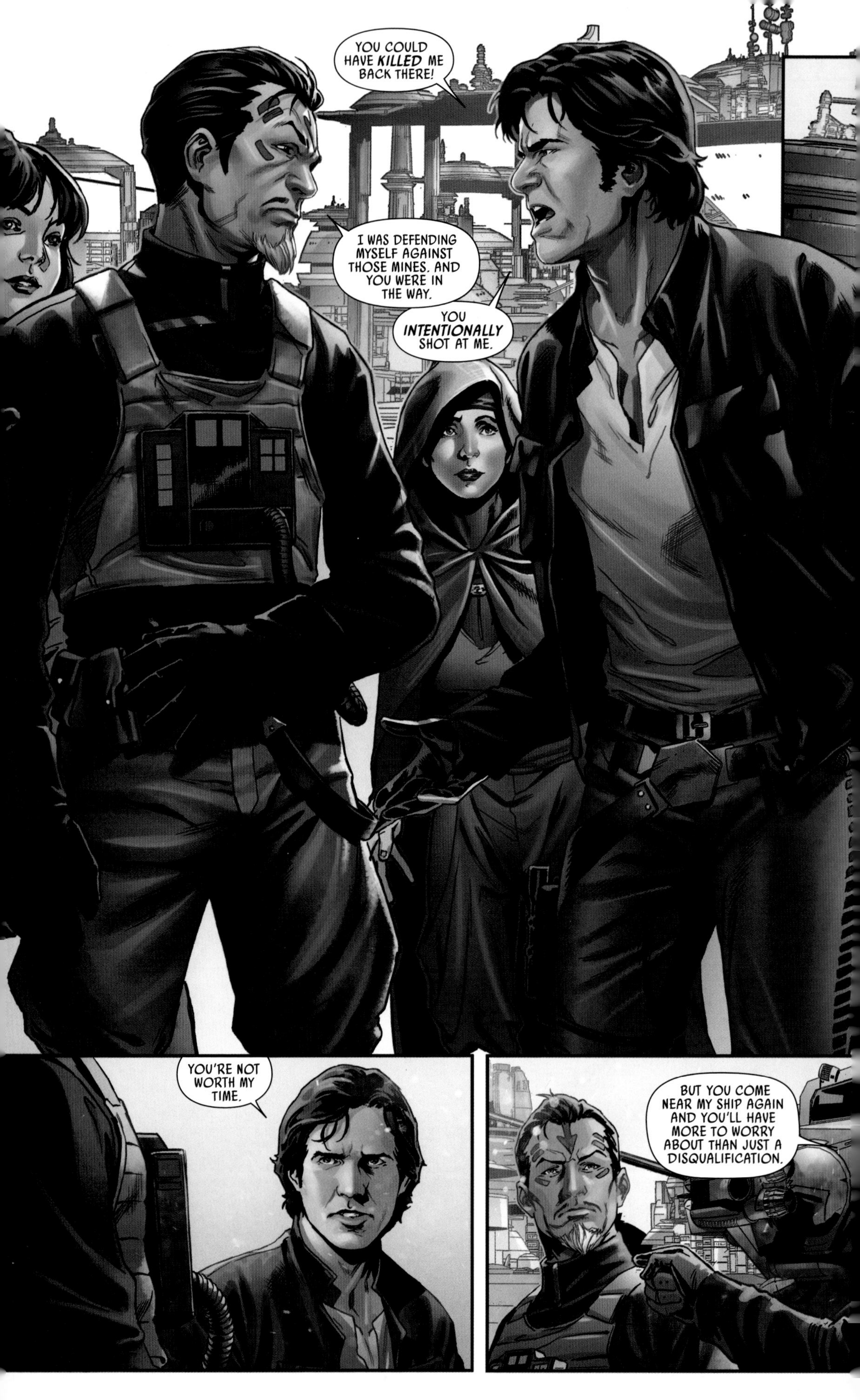
YOU COULD HAVE KILLED ME BACK THERE!
I WAS DEFENDING MYSELF AGAINST THOSE MINES. AND YOU WERE IN THE WAY.
YOU INTENTIONALLY SHOT AT ME.
YOU'RE NOT WORTH MY TIME.
BUT YOU COME NEAR MY SHIP AGAIN AND YOU'LL HAVE MORE TO WORRY ABOUT THAN JUST A DISQUALIFICATION.

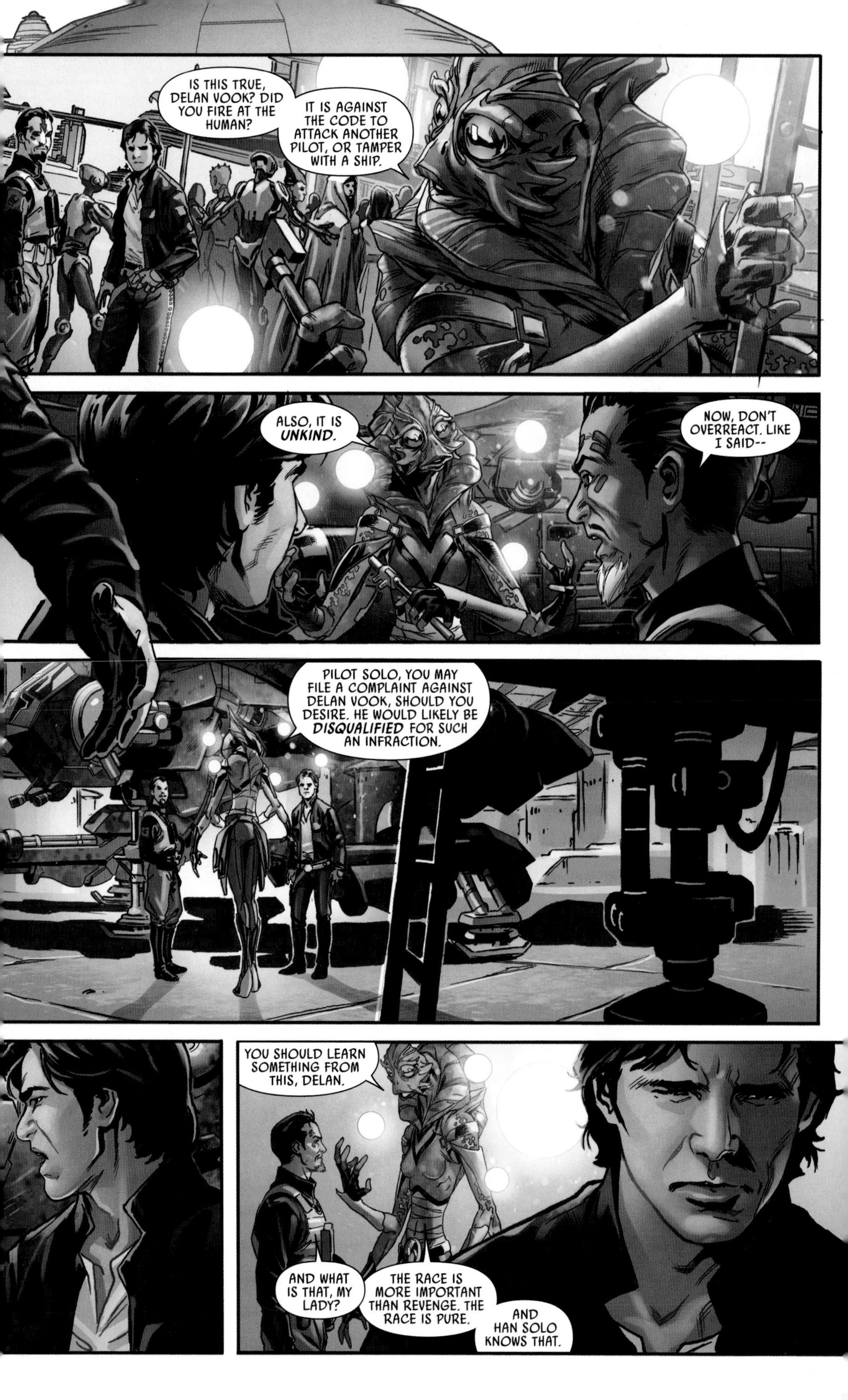
IS THIS TRUE, DELAN VOOK? DID YOU FIRE AT THE HUMAN?
IT IS AGAINST THE CODE TO ATTACK ANOTHER PILOT, OR TAMPER WITH A SHIP.
ALSO, IT IS UNKIND.
NOW, DON'T OVERREACT. LIKE I SAID--
PILOT SOLO, YOU MAY FILE A COMPLAINT AGAINST DELAN VOOK, SHOULD YOU DESIRE. HE WOULD LIKELY BE DISQUALIFIED FOR SUCH AN INFRACTION.
YOU SHOULD LEARN SOMETHING FROM THIS, DELAN.
AND WHAT IS THAT, MY LADY?
THE RACE IS MORE IMPORTANT THAN REVENGE. THE RACE IS PURE.
AND HAN SOLO KNOWS THAT.

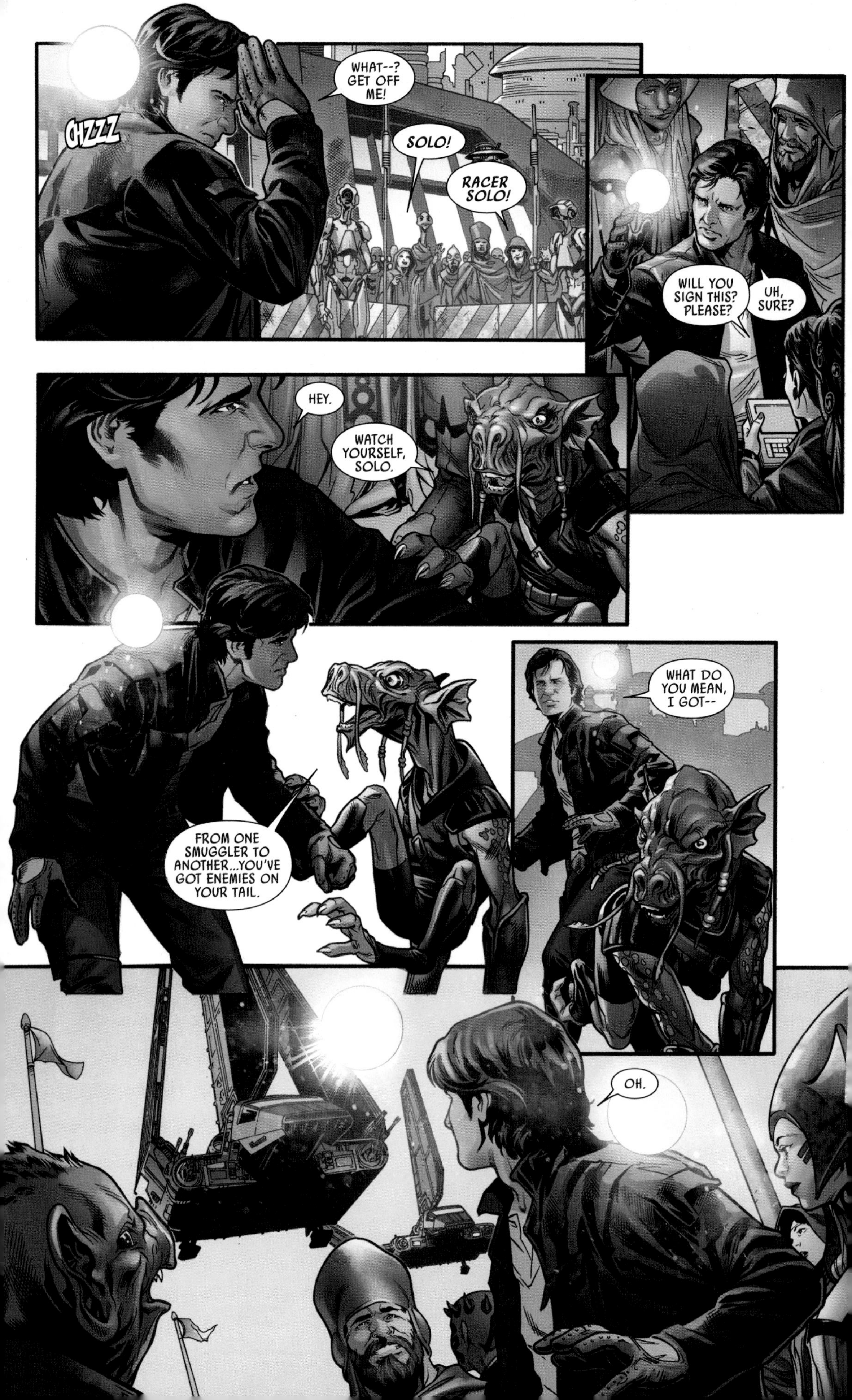
CHZZZ
WHAT--? GET OFF ME!
SOLO!
RACER SOLO!
WILL YOU SIGN THIS? PLEASE?
UH, SURE?
HEY.
WATCH YOURSELF, SOLO.
FROM ONE SMUGGLER TO ANOTHER...YOU'VE GOT ENEMIES ON YOUR TAIL.
WHAT DO YOU MEAN, I GOT--
OH.

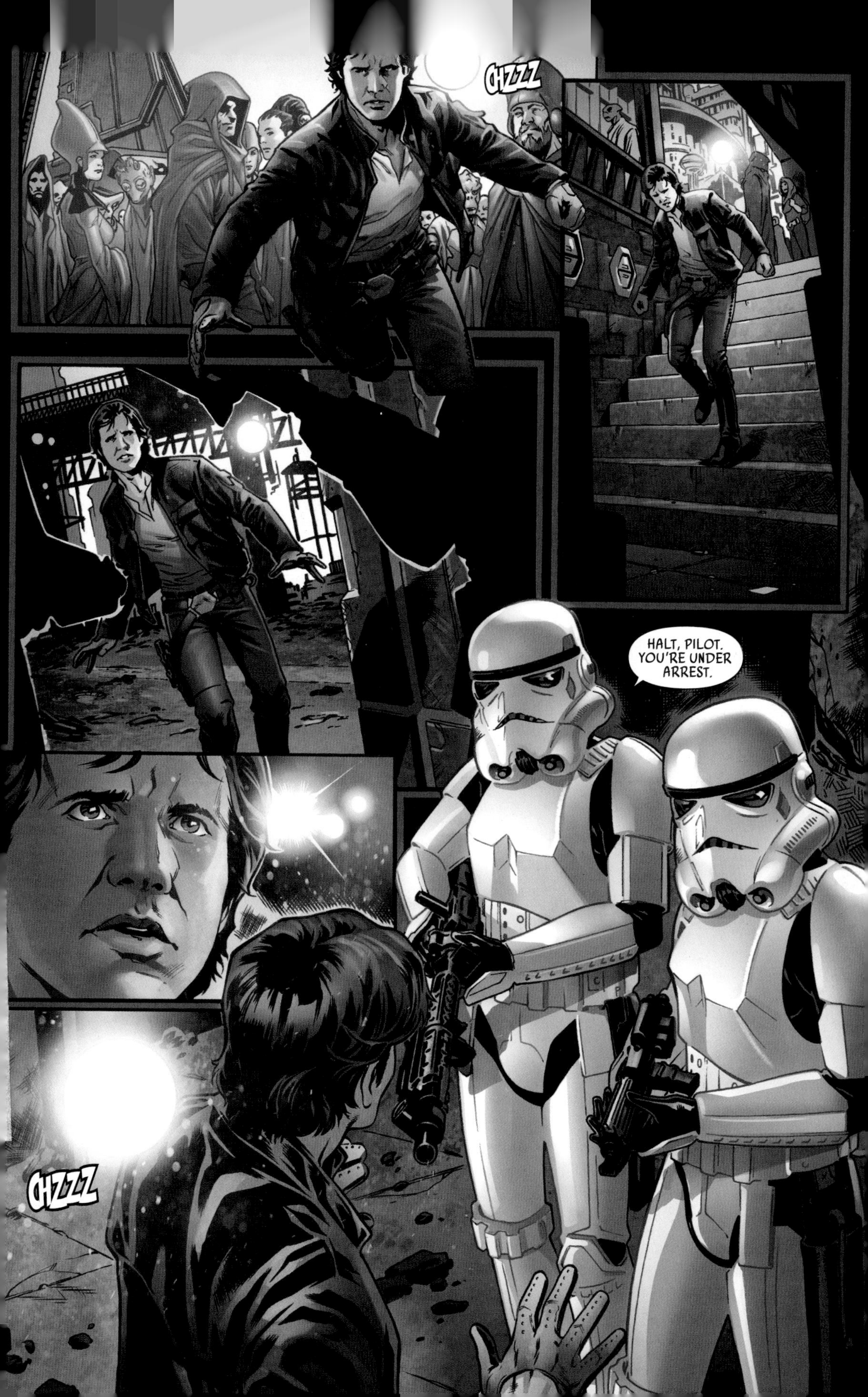
CHZZZ
HALT, PILOT. YOU'RE UNDER ARREST.
CHZZZ

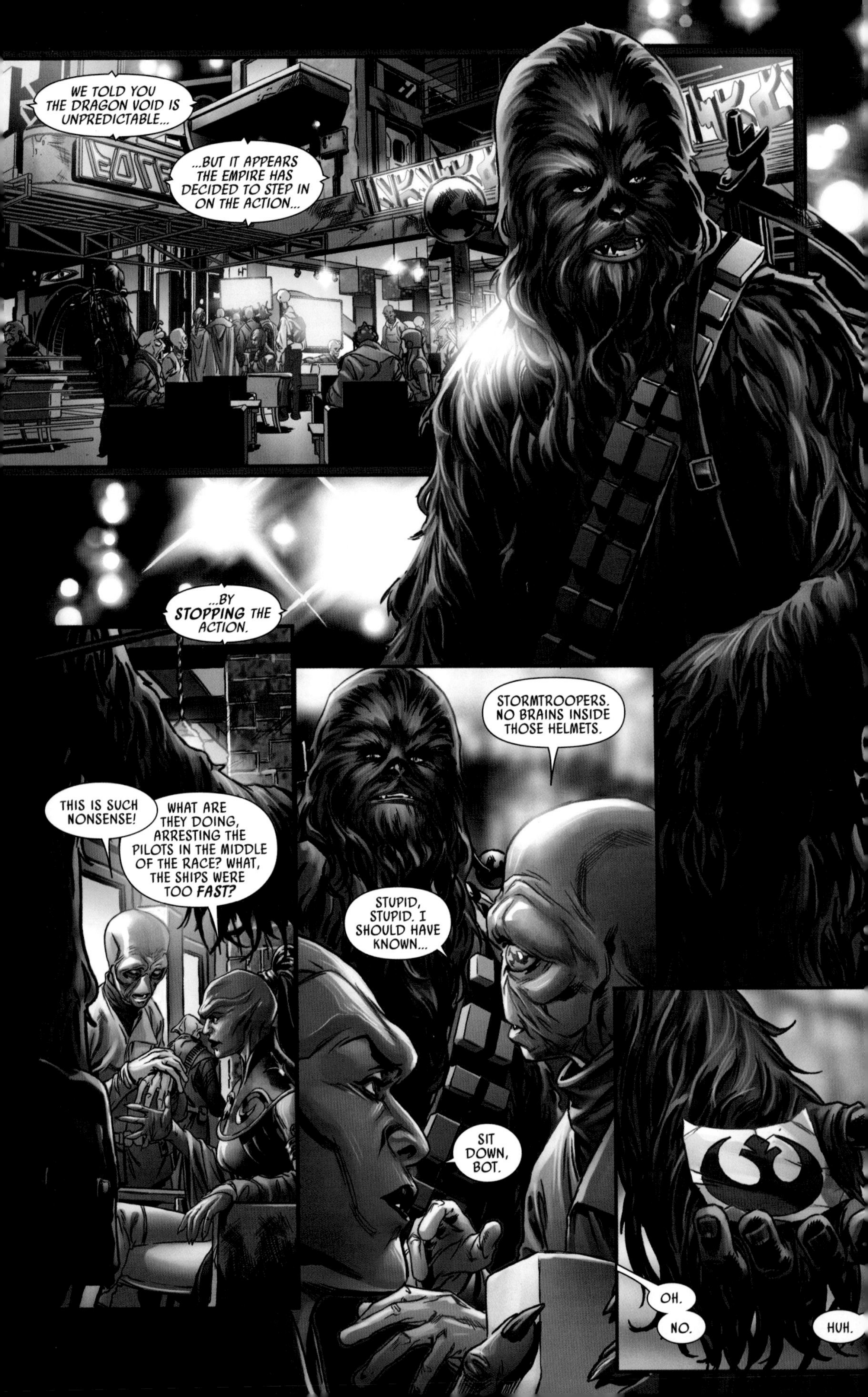
WE TOLD YOU THE DRAGON VOID IS UNPREDICTABLE...
...BUT IT APPEARS THE EMPIRE HAS DECIDED TO STEP IN ON THE ACTION...
...BY STOPPING THE ACTION.
STORMTROOPERS. NO BRAINS INSIDE THOSE HELMETS.
THIS IS SUCH NONSENSE!
WHAT ARE THEY DOING, ARRESTING THE PILOTS IN THE MIDDLE OF THE RACE? WHAT, THE SHIPS WERE TOO FAST?
STUPID, STUPID. I SHOULD HAVE KNOWN...
SIT DOWN, BOT.
OH.
NO.
HUH.

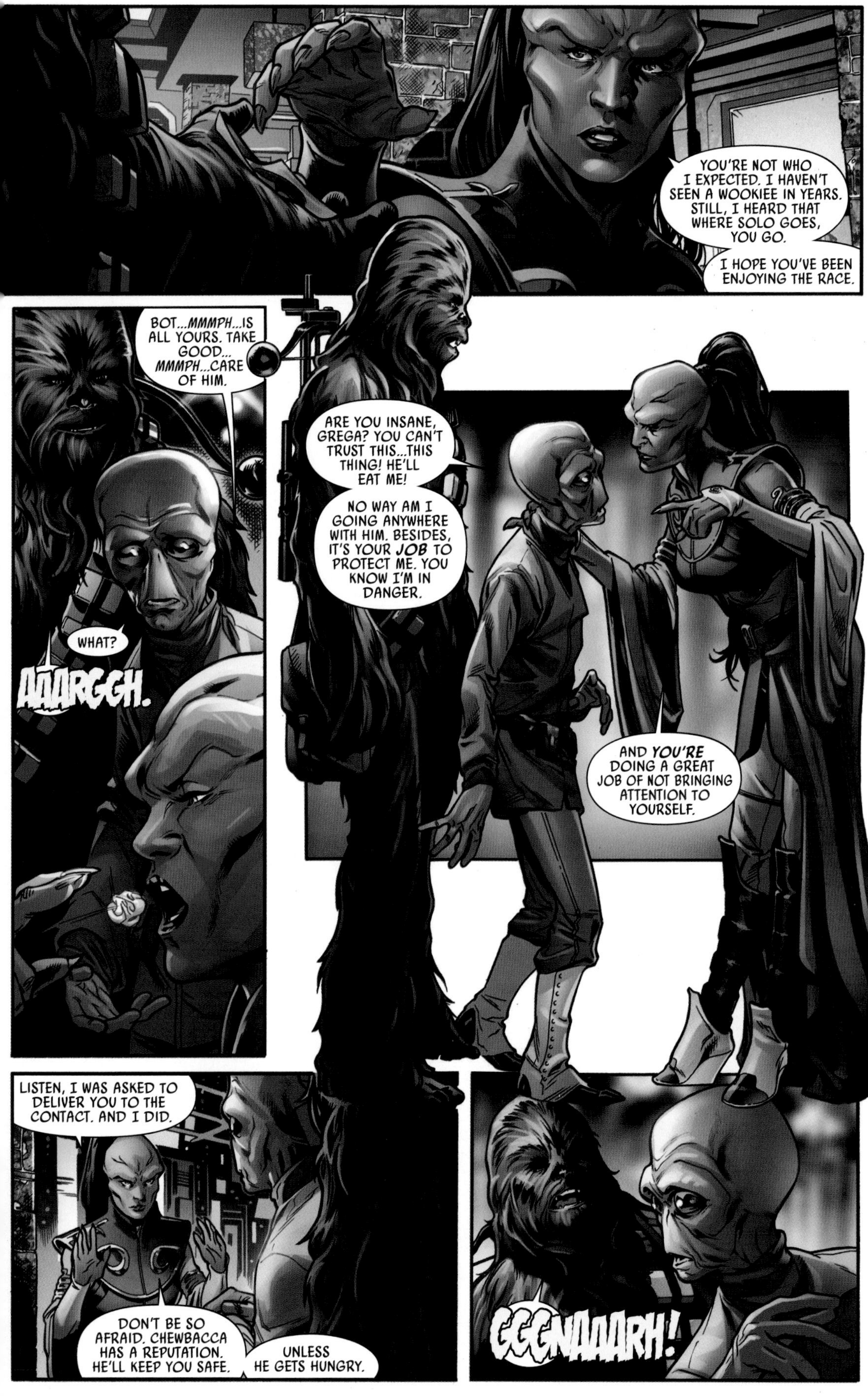
YOU'RE NOT WHO I EXPECTED. I HAVEN'T SEEN A WOOKIEE IN YEARS. STILL, I HEARD THAT WHERE SOLO GOES, YOU GO.
I HOPE YOU'VE BEEN ENJOYING THE RACE.
BOT...MMMPH...IS ALL YOURS. TAKE GOOD... MMMPH...CARE OF HIM.
WHAT?
AAARGGH.
ARE YOU INSANE, GREGA? YOU CAN'T TRUST THIS...THIS THING! HE'LL EAT ME!
NO WAY AM I GOING ANYWHERE WITH HIM. BESIDES, IT'S YOUR JOB TO PROTECT ME. YOU KNOW I'M IN DANGER.
AND YOU'RE DOING A GREAT JOB OF NOT BRINGING ATTENTION TO YOURSELF.
LISTEN, I WAS ASKED TO DELIVER YOU TO THE CONTACT. AND I DID.
DON'T BE SO AFRAID. CHEWBACCA HAS A REPUTATION. HE'LL KEEP YOU SAFE.
UNLESS HE GETS HUNGRY.
GGGNAAARH!

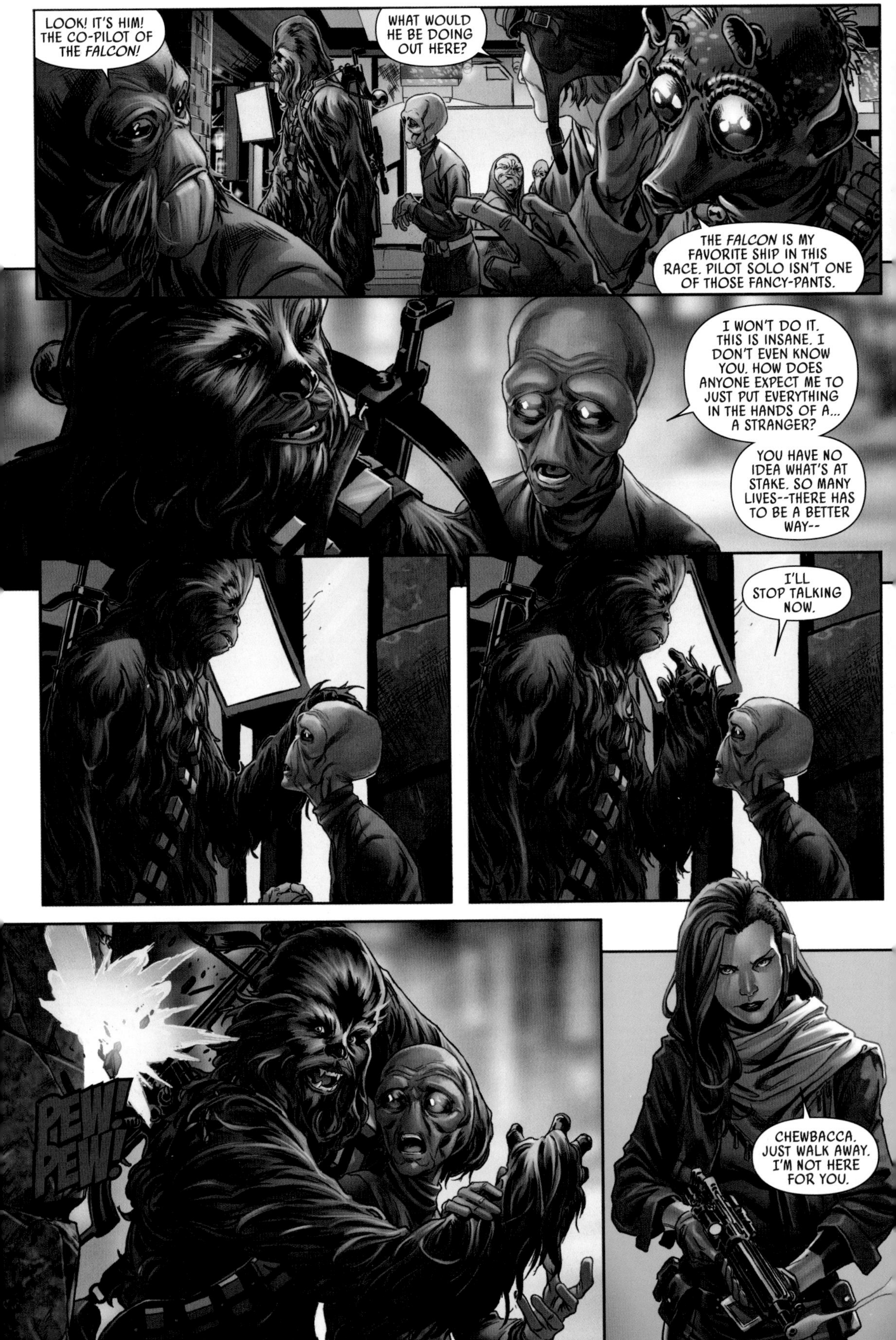
LOOK! IT'S HIM! THE CO-PILOT OF THE FALCON!
WHAT WOULD HE BE DOING OUT HERE?
THE FALCON IS MY FAVORITE SHIP IN THIS RACE. PILOT SOLO ISN'T ONE OF THOSE FANCY-PANTS.
I WON'T DO IT. THIS IS INSANE. I DON'T EVEN KNOW YOU. HOW DOES ANYONE EXPECT ME TO JUST PUT EVERYTHING IN THE HANDS OF A... A STRANGER?
YOU HAVE NO IDEA WHAT'S AT STAKE. SO MANY LIVES--THERE HAS TO BE A BETTER WAY--
I'LL STOP TALKING NOW.
PEW! PEW!
CHEWBACCA. JUST WALK AWAY. I'M NOT HERE FOR YOU.

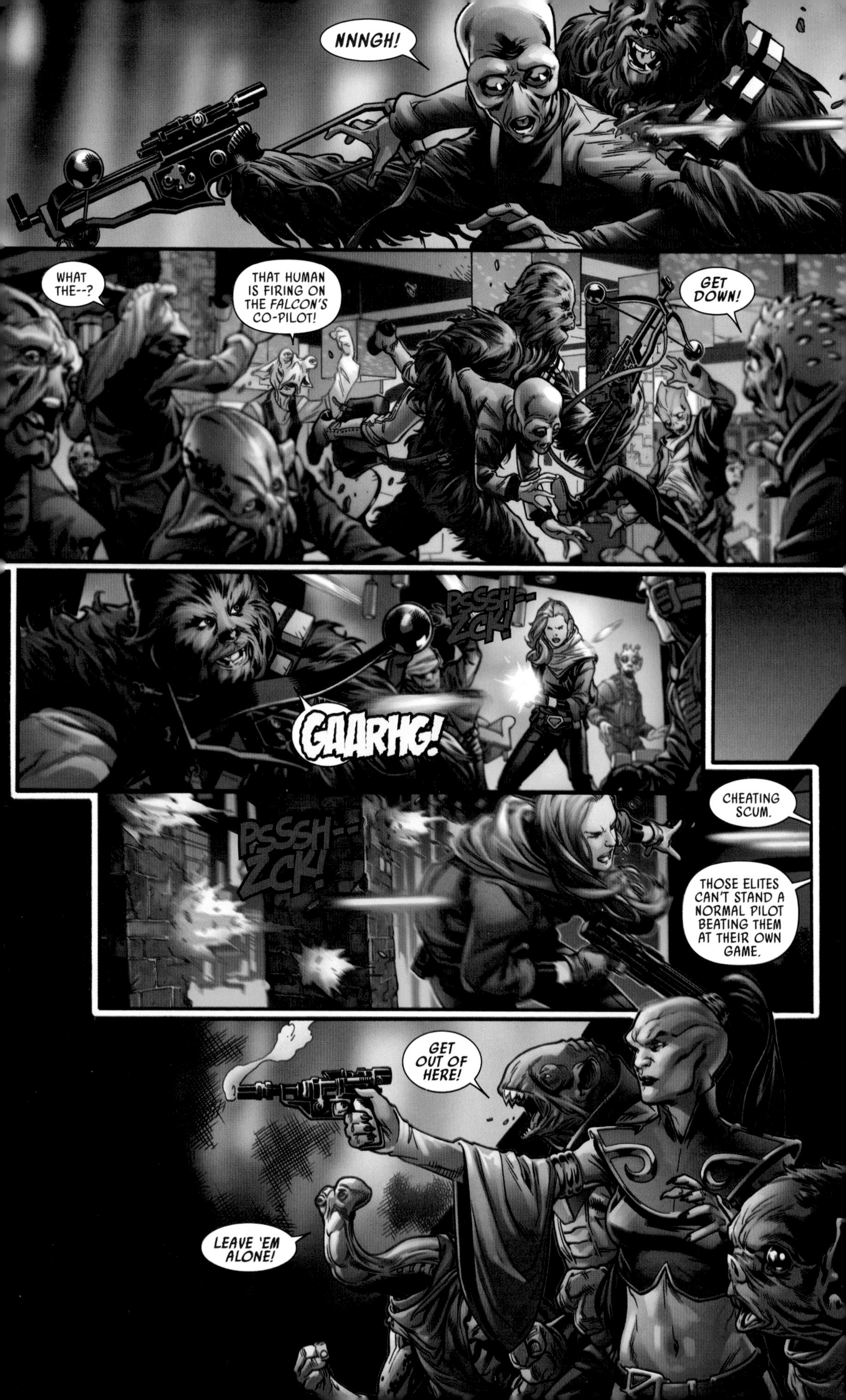
NNNGH!
WHAT THE--?
THAT HUMAN IS FIRING ON THE *FALCON'S* CO-PILOT!
GET DOWN!
PSSSH--ZCK!
GAARHG!
PSSSH--ZCK!
CHEATING SCUM.
THOSE ELITES CAN'T STAND A NORMAL PILOT BEATING THEM AT THEIR OWN GAME.
GET OUT OF HERE!
LEAVE 'EM ALONE!

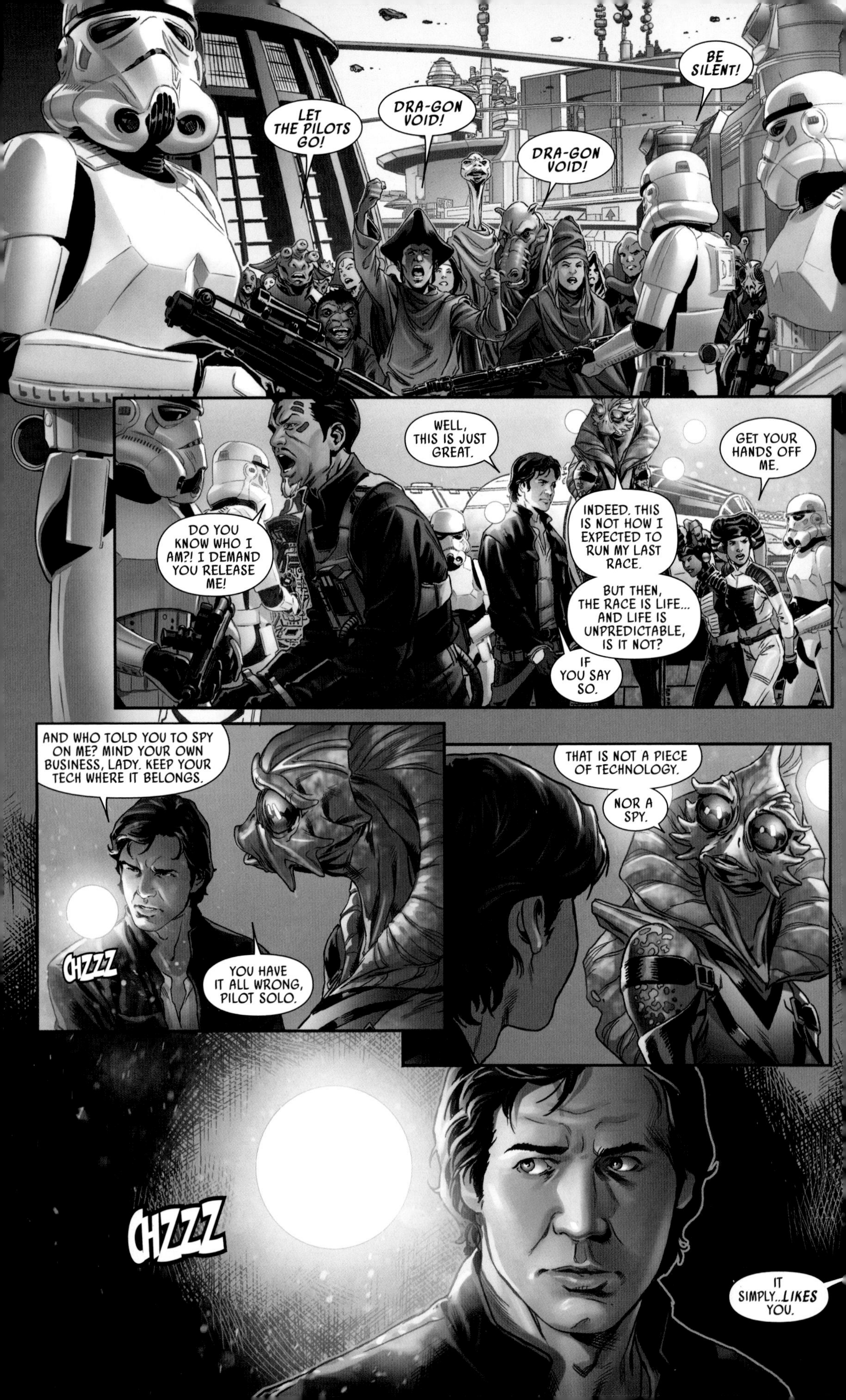
LET THE PILOTS GO!
DRA-GON VOID!
DRA-GON VOID!
BE SILENT!
DO YOU KNOW WHO I AM?! I DEMAND YOU RELEASE ME!
WELL, THIS IS JUST GREAT.
INDEED. THIS IS NOT HOW I EXPECTED TO RUN MY LAST RACE.
BUT THEN, THE RACE IS LIFE... AND LIFE IS UNPREDICTABLE, IS IT NOT?
IF YOU SAY SO.
GET YOUR HANDS OFF ME.
AND WHO TOLD YOU TO SPY ON ME? MIND YOUR OWN BUSINESS, LADY. KEEP YOUR TECH WHERE IT BELONGS.
CHZZZ
YOU HAVE IT ALL WRONG, PILOT SOLO.
THAT IS NOT A PIECE OF TECHNOLOGY.
NOR A SPY.
CHZZZ
IT SIMPLY...LIKES YOU.

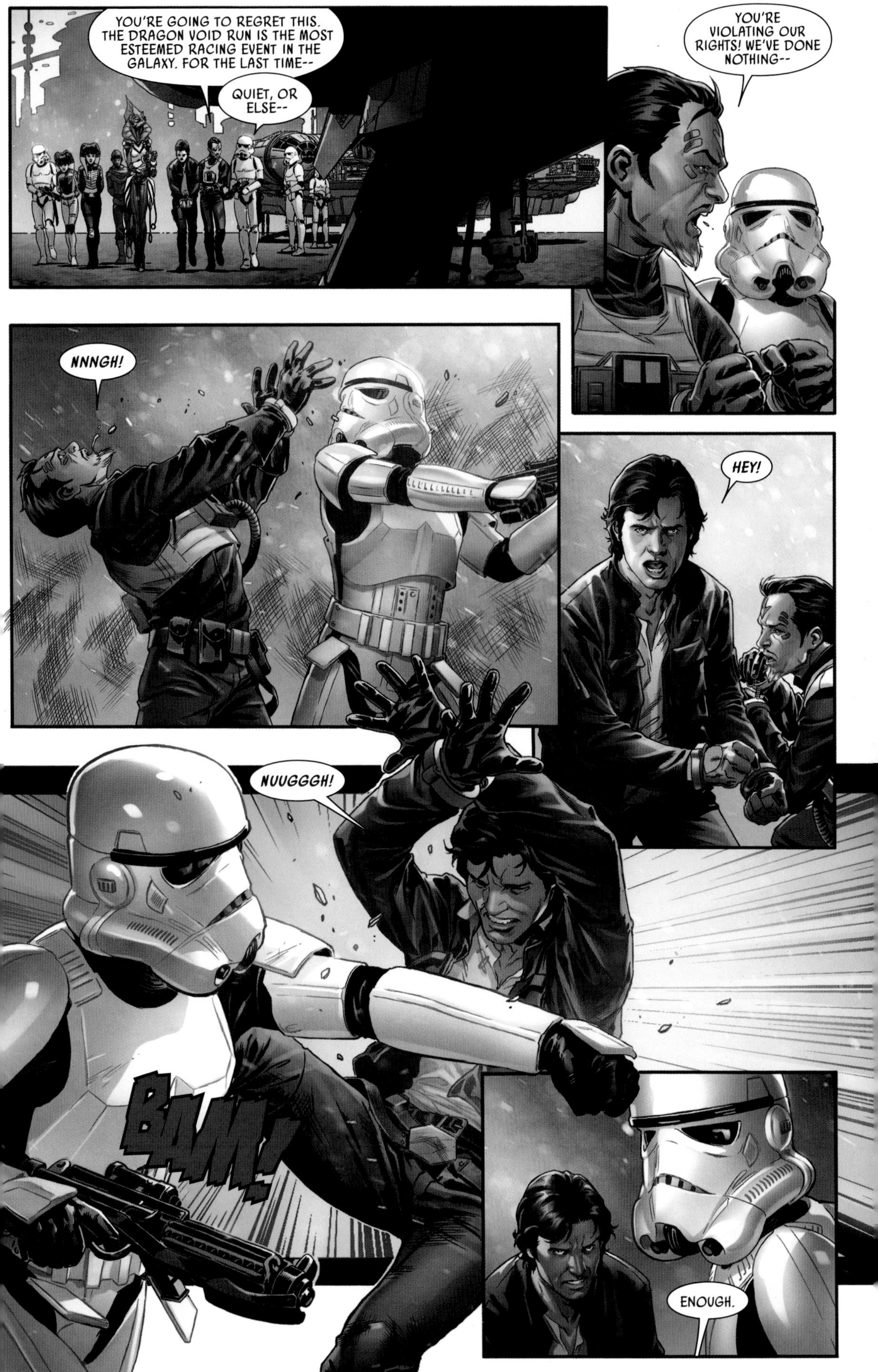
YOU'RE GOING TO REGRET THIS. THE DRAGON VOID RUN IS THE MOST ESTEEMED RACING EVENT IN THE GALAXY. FOR THE LAST TIME--
QUIET, OR ELSE--
YOU'RE VIOLATING OUR RIGHTS! WE'VE DONE NOTHING--
NNNGH!
HEY!
NUUGGGH!
BAM!
ENOUGH.

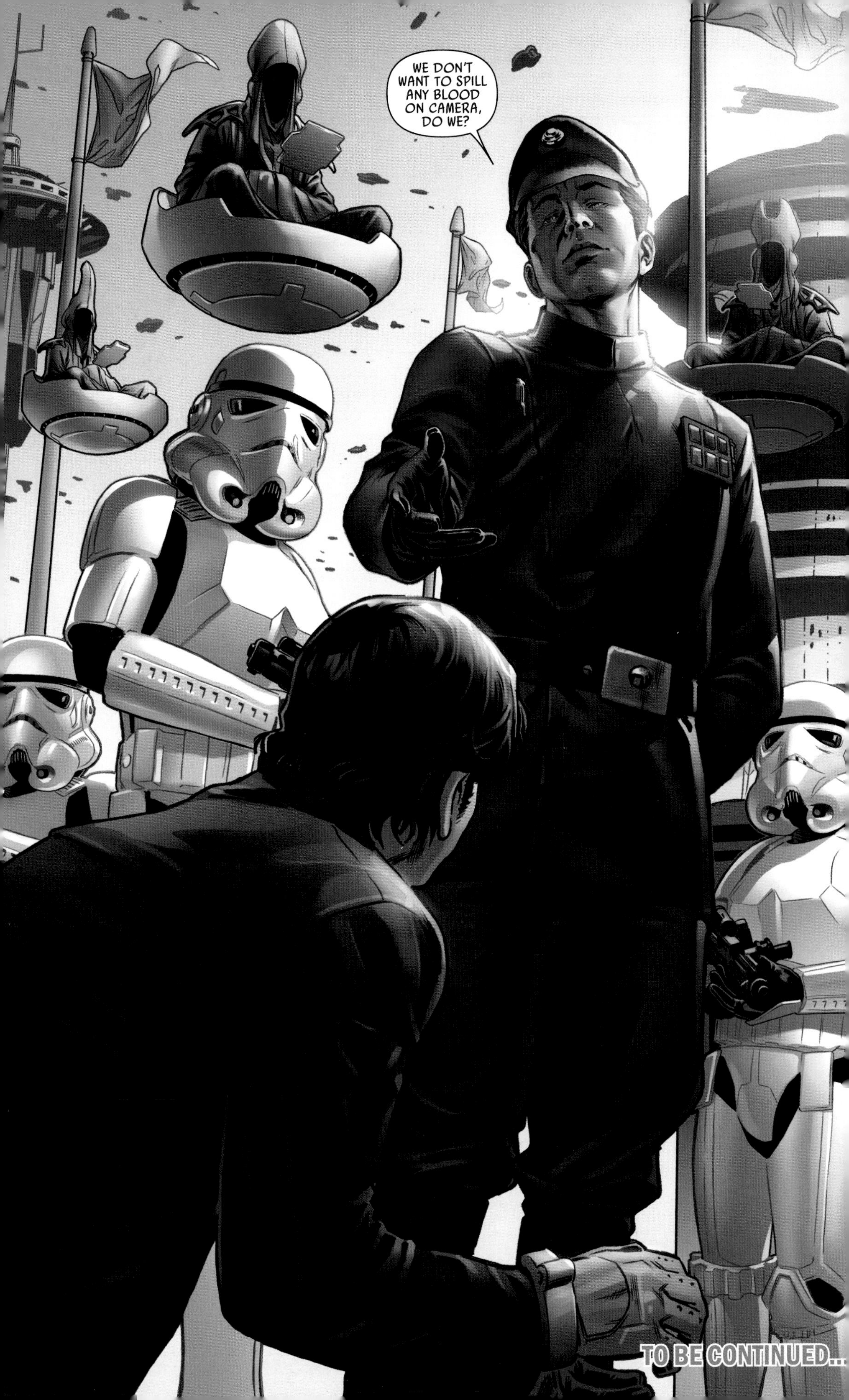
WE DON'T WANT TO SPILL ANY BLOOD ON CAMERA, DO WE?
TO BE CONTINUED...

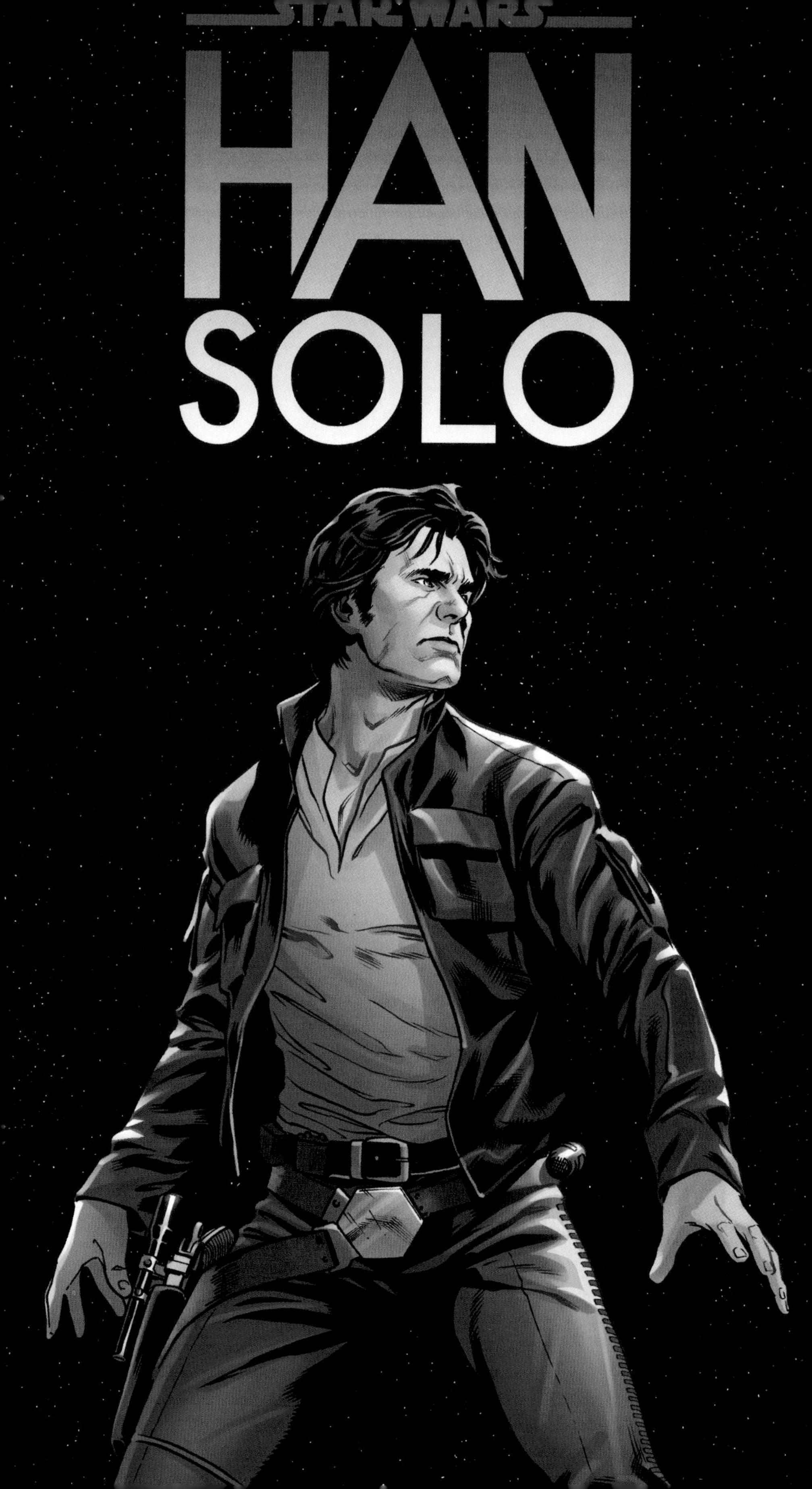
STAR WARS
HAN
SOLO

STAR WARS

HAN SOLO

COLLECT THEM ALL!

Set of 5 Hardcover Books ISBN: 978-1-5321-4014-

STAR WARS
STAR WARS
HAN SOLO
HAN SOLO: VOLUME 1
LIU BROOKS OBACK

Hardcover Book ISBN
978-1-5321-4015-0

STAR WARS
STAR WARS
HAN SOLO
HAN SOLO: VOLUME 2
LIU BROOKS OBACK

Hardcover Book ISBN
978-1-5321-4016-7

STAR WARS
STAR WARS
SOLO
HAN SOLO: VOLUME 3
LIU BROOKS OBACK

Hardcover Book ISBN
978-1-5321-4017-4

STAR WARS
STAR WARS
HAN SOLO
HAN SOLO: VOLUME 4
LIU BROOKS OBACK MILLA

Hardcover Book ISBN
978-1-5321-4018-1

STAR WARS
STAR WARS
HAN SOLO
HAN SOLO: VOLUME 5
LIU BROOKS OBACK

Hardcover Book ISBN
978-1-5321-4019-8